Parent's Introduction

Whether your child is a beginning reader, a reluctant reader, or an eager reader, this book offers a fun and easy way to encourage and help your child in reading.

Developed with reading education specialists, *We Both Read* books invite you and your child to take turns reading aloud. You read the left-hand pages of the book, and your child reads the right-hand pages—which have been written at one of six early reading levels. The result is a wonderful new reading experience and faster reading development!

You may find it helpful to read the entire book aloud yourself the first time, then invite your child to participate the second time. As you read, try to make the story come alive by reading with expression. This will help to model good fluency. It will also be helpful to stop at various points to discuss what you are reading. This will help increase your child's understanding of what is being read.

In some books, a few challenging words are introduced in the parent's text, distinguished with **bold** lettering. Pointing out and discussing these words can help to build your child's reading vocabulary. If your child is a beginning reader, it may be helpful to run a finger under the text as each of you reads. Please also notice that a "talking parent" ☺ icon precedes the parent's text, and a "talking child" ☺ icon precedes the child's text.

If your child struggles with a word, you can encourage "sounding it out," but keep in mind that not all words can be sounded out. Your child might pick up clues about a word from the picture, other words in the sentence, or any rhyming patterns. If your child struggles with a word for more than five seconds, it is usually best to simply say the word.

Most of all, remember to praise your child's efforts and keep the reading fun. After you have finished the book, ask a few questions and discuss what you have read together. Rereading this book multiple times may also be helpful for your child.

Try to keep the tips above in mind as you read together, but don't worry about doing everything right. Simply sharing the enjoyment of reading together will increase your child's reading skills and help to start your child off on a lifetime of reading enjoyment!

The Ant
and
The Pancake

A We Both Read Book
Level K–1
Guided Reading: Level C

Text Copyright © 2010, 2015 by Treasure Bay, Inc.

By Paul Orshoski and Dave Max
Adapted by Sindy McKay

Illustrations Copyright © 2010 by Jeffrey Ebbeler

This book is based in part on the We Read Phonics books *How to Make a Pancake* and *Ant in Her Pants*, but this book has been significantly revised and adapted for the We Both Read shared-reading format. You may find the We Read Phonics versions to be complementary and helpful companions to this title.

Reading Consultant: Bruce Johnson, M.Ed.

We Both Read® is a trademark of Treasure Bay, Inc.

Published by Treasure Bay, Inc.
P.O. Box 119
Novato, CA 94948 USA

Printed in Malaysia

Library of Congress Catalog Card Number: 2014944093

ISBN: 978-1-60115-272-5

Visit us online at WeBothRead.com

PR-10-18

The Ant

By Paul Orshoski

Adapted by Sindy McKay

Illustrated by Jeffrey Ebbeler

TREASURE BAY

Miss Grant had a nice pair of pants which attracted a curious ant.

This ant gave Miss Grant quite a shock when the ant came and ran . . .

2

. . . up her sock.

The ant ate up all of her lunch.
Then he slurped down her whole . . .

. . . box of punch.

He climbed all the way to her chin, where he thanked her and gave . . .

. . . her a grin.

He headed back down to her slacks,
and it itched as he walked . . .

. . . down her back.

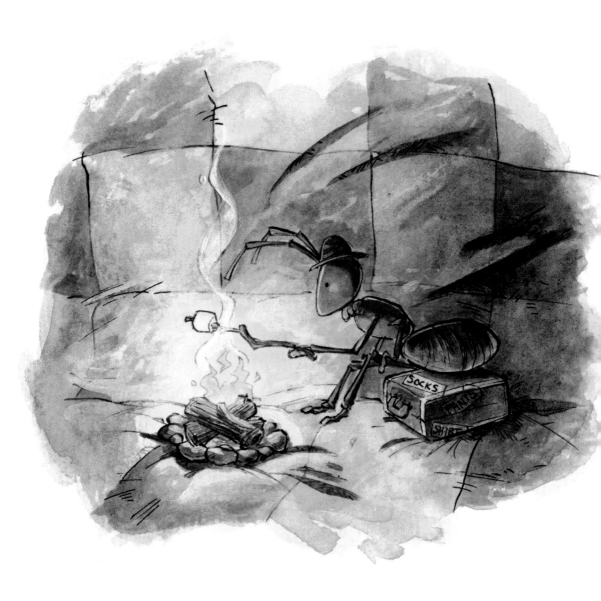

She stopped and she felt a hot burn.
So she hopped and she made . . .

. . . a fast turn.

She ran till she fell with a thud.
And her pants were all covered . . .

. . . in mud.

The ant liked his songs with a beat.
And Miss Grant's pretty pants felt . . .

 . . . the heat!

She jumped off the dock and got wet.
Then she sloshed up the street . . .

 . . . to a vet.

The vet said, "Those pants have to go," but Miss Grant shook her head . . .

. . . and said, "No!"

Miss Grant is still wearing those pants.
And she never got rid of . . .

. . . that ant.

WE BOTH READ®

The Pancake

By Dave Max

Edited and Adapted by Sindy McKay

Illustrated by Jeffrey Ebbeler

TREASURE BAY

Would you like to make a pancake? Great!
Who can you ask to help? How about . . .

 . . . Mom or Dad!

 If they are too busy, maybe you can ask some nice mice to help. The first thing you will need . . .

 . . . is an egg.

Measure out a cup of pancake mix. Then crack the egg in a dish.

Mix well.

Now carefully add the pancake mix to the egg.

Mix it up.

Add in a cup of milk and use a whisk to blend it all together. Try not to . . .

. . . make a mess!

You now have pancake batter that's ready to cook.
Next have your parent or a helpful mouse melt
some butter . . .

34

. . . in a pan.

Now have Mom or Dad pour a bit of the batter into the hot, buttered pan. Keep your eye on the batter.

Is it wet?

When the batter no longer looks wet, it's time to flip the pancake! Once it's fully cooked, you can take it from the pan and put it . . .

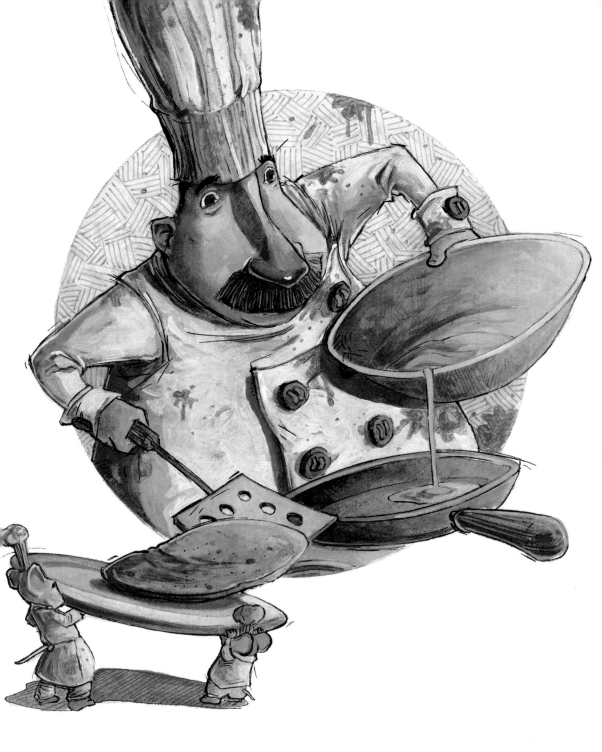

. . . on a plate.

Make a big stack, and smear it with some butter. You
might ask Mom or Dad to cut up a plum to put . . .

. . . on top.

Now it's time to dig in and eat! Be sure to share with Mom or Dad—or some nice mice. But be careful not to eat too many or you just may need . . .

42

. . . a nap!

If you liked **The Ant and The Pancake**, here is another
We Both Read® book you are sure to enjoy!

The Mouse in My House

A boy does everything he can to catch a mouse
in this zany and funny tale. The smart little mouse
seems to be having the time of his life evading
capture until suddenly he is scooped into a jar and
carried off far from home. However, the mouse
gets the last laugh as he finds his way back home
and takes over the house with a lot of his furry
little friends.

To see all the We Both Read books that are available,
just go online to **www.WeBothRead.com**.